A First-Start® Easy Reader

This easy reader contains only 53 different words,
repeated often to help the young reader develop
word recognition and interest in reading.

Basic word list for *Christmas Surprise*

it	ran	she
was	and	Christmas
I	down	morning
of	wake	jumped
the	stairs	everybody
up	said	Santa
or	here	forget
did	room	forgets
he	door	forgot
into	yes	living
at	Mom	through
a	Dad	never
for	but	looked
you	need	presents
is	what	present
me	just	there
out	this	thank
bed		about

Christmas Surprise

Written by Sharon Gordon

Illustrated by John Magine

Troll Associates

It was Christmas morning.

I jumped out of bed.

I ran down the stairs.

"Wake up, everybody!

Wake up!" I said.

"Was Santa here?

Or did he forget?"

I ran into the living room.

I ran through the door.

"Yes. Santa was here.

Santa never forgets."

I looked at the presents.

There was a present for Mom.

"Thank you, Santa," she said.

"This is just what I need."

There was a present for Dad.

"Thank you, Santa," he said.

"This is just what I need."

"But what about me?" I said.

"Did Santa forget me?

Did Santa forget a present for me?"

There was a present for Mom.

There was a present for Dad.

But Santa forgot a present for me.

"Here is a present for you," said Mom and Dad.

"Santa never forgets."

"Thank you, Santa," I said.

"This is just what I need!"